IMAGINE THAT

Licensed exclusively to Imagine That Publishing Ltd
Tide Mill Way, Woodbridge, Suffolk, IP12 1AP, UK
www.imaginethat.com
Copyright © 2019 Imagine That Group Ltd
All rights reserved
2 4 6 8 9 7 5 3 1
Manufactured in China

Written by Joshua George
Illustrated by Sarah Lawrence

ISBN 978-1-78700-912-7

A catalogue record for this book is available from the British Library

For Dad, thanks for all the bedtime stories

ROAR!
went the lion

by **Joshua George**
& **Sarah Lawrence**

'Roar!' went the lion ...

Baa! went the cow ...

Moo! went the wolf ...

'**Oink!**' went the owl ...

'Twit-twoo!'
went the pig ...

'**Cluck!**' went the frog ...

'Awoooo!'
went the sheep ...

'Bzzzz!' went the dog ...

'**Ribbit!**' went the bee ...

Woof!
went the hen ...

'**Stop, stop!**
You've got it
all wrong, let's
start again!'

'Awoooo!'
went the wolf ...

'Twit twoo!' went the owl ...

'Oink!
went the pig ...

'Ribbit!

went the frog ...

'**Baa!**'
went the sheep ...

Woof! went the dog ...

Bzzz!
went the bee ...

'**Cluck!**'
went the hen ...

'Goodness me, what was all that noise? Now please be quiet and go to sleep!'

'Roar!' went the lion ...

'Yay, let's start again!'